Sabinah's Poetry -Her Travels

VOLUME ONE

No copyright infringement is intended

Editor: Patsy Middleton
Sub-editor: Dianne Jones

ISBN paperback: 978-1-8381699-5-4

Contents

The Leopard 🐆 Coat of many Colours #301

The leopard in its beauty
The coat of tranquility
The spread of variety

Vastness in its pride
Strength in its stride
Greatness in its tribe

The coat of colours
The different creatures
The gift of nature

Leos are lions
Snakes are dangerous
Leopards are glamorous

The spots its valour
The speed its amour
The leopard of power

Inspired to write about the leopard
Composed on the train and finished at the hairdresser on
14/02/20

Bleeding Rose 🌷 #302

Roses are red
Roses have thorns

The beauty of a rose
Is in contrast with the thorn
The beauty of a relationship
Can be measured in roses

The thorn of a rose can pierce an open heart
The sweetest heart

A broken heart is like the pain felt from the rose's thorn
The petals of roses wither away with time
The thorns last a long time

The blood that was shed when He died on the cross for me and you
The blood from the petals cannot mend a broken heart

But He shed His blood to heal our pain
The petals can bleed from the thorns but the blood will heal our
pain

#Queen of Poems Challenge
Composed for the Queen of Poems Challenge

The Death Cafe #303 #Live

Life is for the living
Live and let live
Live for today

Learning of the death of a sister
Grief in my heart for a sister
A and E is a disaster

Families visiting with loved ones
Queues forming all night long
Pains unimaginable for too long

Eating and drinking
Dancing and dining
Wining and celebrating

Life is too short
Dining might stop short
Life may be cut short

Live and let live

Composed at the hairdresser
Inspired to write following the death of a sister on 14/02/2020

Work Meet Connect #304

Work work work
All work but no play
Makes Jack a long day

Link makes us connect
To impact makes us connect
Waves make a better connection

Meeting at a service
Meet to socialise
Meet to fuel your energy

Work connection has lasting affection
Fuel at a service has a lasting effect
Connecting gives a lasting impression

Work Meet Connect

Inspired to write about the plague at the service
Composed at the wedding on 15/02/2020

Peacock at the Wedding #305

We arrived at the wedding
We arrived at the venue
We arrived at the hall

Guests were sitting
Guests were standing
Guests were chatting

Weather was raining
Weather was pouring
Weather was spitting

Watching the outdoors
Windows were beautiful
Windows were decorated

Looking through
Watching through
Picking through

Gravel crunching
Peacock snooping
Water logging

Conversing with peacock
Beauty with peacock
Watching with peacock

Invited peacock at the wedding
What's the strangest guest at the wedding?

Composed at the hotel on 15/02/2020
Inspired to write about the peacock at the wedding

Interlocking Mirrors #306

It was at Farnham
Yes it was at Frensham
The hotel at the farmland

The reception full of artifacts
The history reminds you of facts
India played on the facts

The mirror on the wall
Had circles all around
That interlock in rounds

The world goes around
In circles we go around
The mirror goes around

Have you been in a circle
Life goes round in circles
We need to break the cycle

Follow the circles in a circle
One circle leads to another circle
Circle after cycle

We need to break the cycle
The interlocking mirror

Composed at home in my room on 16/02/20
Inspired to write about the mirror

The Buddhist #307

Arriving at the hotel
Reception welcome
Buddhist welcome

Checked in online
Keys in line
Luggage in line

Walking on the grounds
Relax on my grounds
White image on the rounds

The relax
The calm
The unwind

Restored in nature
Green restructure
Lake in the structure

Prayer mode
Unwinds the mode
Walkers with mode

The Buddhist welcome

Composed at home on my day off
Inspired to write about the Buddhist in the hotel 17/02/2020

Split Image #308

Suicide on my mind
Amy Winehouse

In the library on my journey
What an image in a vibrant area
Children everywhere

Brings memories of
Caroline Flack

Suicide on my mind
Celebrities on my mind
Anyone on my mind
Split images

Could mean a line on your face
Could mean a line in your heart
Could mean a split in your heart
Could mean a knife in your heart

The mosque on my mind
A knife in my mind
A split image in my heart
A split second in my heart
Split image could trigger a split in my mind

Composed at home in my room on 22/02/2020
Inspired to write about the drawing on the wall

Holidays #309 #Rejuvenate #Revitalise

The sun is out
The children are out

The boat sets sail
The waves help it sail

The umbrellas keep out the tan
The sunshine brings out your tan

The birds flying high
The sky setting high

The blue in the sea
The blue in the sky

The boat in its stride
The sea in its pride

All set for fun
All set for sun

Holidays

Composed in my room on 25/02/20
Inspired to write about the picture

The Eagle 310 # Strength #Leadership

The Eagle with its beak
60 species of the beat
Eurasia and Africa its fleet

The Eagle flies high
The Eagle flies alone
The Eagle flies in strength

The Eagle is a leader
The Eagle is very strong
The Eagle has the best sight

Eyes are powerful
Beak is strong for catching prey
Wings are mighty as it flies

25

King of birds
Strong sturdy legs
Powerful talons

Eagles do not mix
Prefer to fly alone
Unique in its flight

Eagle of beauty
Eagle of majesty
Eagle of tranquility

Eagle of totality
Eagle of fullness
Eagle of altitude

The Eagle

Composed at home on 26/02/20
Inspired to write about the eagle

The Mask #311

What is this on your face
What is this on your fate
What is this on your ninja

The mask to protect
The mask to reduce
The mask for life

The mask for doctors
The mask the protector
The mask across the globe

Green is its colour
White is a collar
Filtered is its honour

Great is thy mask
Scarce is its mark
Hope is its farce

The Mask

Composed on the train
Inspired to write about the mask on 27/02/20

E-cigarettes #312

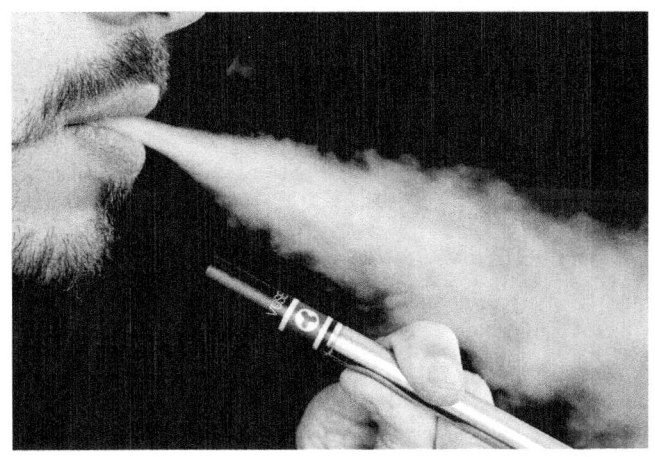

E-cigarettes
Vapour smoking for relaxation
Sushi smoking for socialisation
Smoking for consideration
Which one do you belong to?

Safer smoking
To protect our children from harm
To protect our homes from fires
To protect our families from sorrows
Fires break out from smoking

The E-cigarette may be safer
The sellers are trying their best
The manufacturers are doing their bit

But what are we doing as parents
So many still smoke indoors—endangering lives
Some still smoke in cars—endangering passengers

480,000 deaths a year in the USA through cigarette smoking
41,000 deaths a year through second-hand exposure
Current youth and young adults; 63% did not know the product
contains nicotine
Smokers die 10 years earlier than non-smokers

In the U.K. no vaping related deaths have been confirmed
Vaping has been heralded as a healthier alternative to smoking
cigarettes
Allows you to inhale nicotine as vapour rather than breathing in
smoke

What will you do?

Composed in A and E on 28/02/2020
Inspired to write about tobacco safer smoking

Pop N Bowl #313

Mum's anniversary
Nice atmosphere
Joined me at the parlour

Colleagues leaving do
Bring back memories of fun times
Bowling and dining

Bumped into work colleague
Half-term week
Popcorn on the menu

Nachos for two
Wine on the house
Steak and burger

Families having fun
Bowling away
Children having fun

Fun for all
Pop N Bowl

Inspired to write about the bowling parlour
Composed in Subway on 02/03/20

Sanitiser #314 Infection control

Hand gel

I went to Superdrug and bought sanitiser for £3.99 each
Two of them for my staff team; due to the coronavirus
We have been advised to buy sanitiser and wash our hands
regularly
We went to Poundland, Savers, Boots—and all the shelves were
empty
We looked online; it was £467 on eBay
It was £99.99 on Amazon; the same sanitiser that I bought two
weeks ago!

Why has it become so expensive
Why has sanitiser become hot cakes
Why has sanitiser become unavailable everywhere
This is because of stockpiling

Why do the businesses believe they can exhort money
From vulnerable people trying to save their lives from viral
infection
Why have things become so entangled

The pharmaceutical companies trying to make money
Why do we panic buy and then some do not have access to
sanitisers
Sanitisers are no longer available anywhere
Sanitiser

Inspired to write this poem due to the scarcity of sanitiser
Composed at home on 04/03/20

Boats on Sail #315

Attending a wedding
On the wall in the hotel; hangs a painting
Reminded me of rowing in the Olympics
Yet this was not the Olympics

The beauty of it is the boats lined up in the distance
The clouds in the background
On a dark cloudy evening

The sea was calm
Yet not blue; but was calm
The boats were sailing in unison
The beauty of the boards sailing
Caught my attention

When next you're in a hotel—watch out
For the picture that stands out in the pile

Boats on sail

Composed on the train on 11/03/20
Inspired to write about the boat painting

Life is a Journey #316

As I was about to leave the ward in Mile End hospital
My attention was caught by the picture

Life is a journey
I thought; and yet life can be taken at any time

With all the patients not sure of what might happen
It's a bit uncertain, I thought

With lives being cut short by what is happening around the world
Life is indeed a journey

We have to make the most of it
Live for today

Hope for tomorrow
Love each other

Love thy neighbour as thyself—is the second commandment
Do you know the first commandment?

Composed on the train on 12/03/20
Inspired to write about the picture on the ward

Cutlery in the Loo 317

It was at the Studio 3 Arts event
I went to use the bathroom

I noticed the cutlery on the wall
The knives, forks and spoons

It was interesting to have this in a toilet, I thought
I saw the loo roll on the side

It was interesting as people were stocking up on toilet rolls
So I thought I could write a poem about the Cutlery in the Loo

So as we continue to stock up
We should remember to wash our hands after using cutlery for
meals

What else has fascinated you on your journey?

The Cutlery in the Loo

Composed in the car on 15/03/2020
Inspired to write about the cutlery in the loo

Ladders #318

Elevate
Lifts you higher
From point A to B

Employment ladder
Move up higher
Gain heights
Withstand pressure
Can take you to places unknown

Ladders
Can we manage without them

Builders rely on them
Step ladders are very handy
They help to gain access to the loft

Ladders
You need them for the top shelves in the kitchen
They give access to the rooftop
To prevent leaks

I saw them on my walk this morning
The workmen on the rooftop
I thought—without the ladders

It makes our lives easier around the home
Be careful as you step up the ladder

Ladders

Composed on the train
Inspired to write about the ladder on 16/03/20

A Strong Woman #319

Attending the school event at Orsett Hall
Saw the painting on the wall

Reminded me of Mona Lisa
Thought she reminded me of a strong woman
Who comes to mind

I thought of myself
I have been through a lot
I have shown my resilience to deal with matters that have affected
me

I have shown my depth to deal with emotional issues
I have shown growth to deal with issues of rejection

When this might not have anything to do with you
I have drawn from my faith; whenever I feel low and have not had
the answers

Strength can be tested any time or day
We have to be prepared that things can change any time
Nothing in life is permanent

A strong woman

Composed on the train on 18/03/20
Inspired to write about the picture on the wall

Social Distancing #320

Avoiding unnecessary contact with other people
No more food on the shelves
Rationing of toilet rolls

Queues as early as 5.40am
Travel disruption
Bow Road Station is shut—limited bus services
No night trains any longer
Timetables on bus routes on Saturdays

Mortgages supported for three months
Driving tests are cancelled
Salaries up to 80% being paid
Cafes, theatres, restaurants and gyms are closing

Avoid gatherings with friends and family
Hairdressers are closed
Weddings are being cancelled
Funerals are being cancelled

Household isolation
Schools are closed
Stay at home
Work from home

Exams are cancelled
Sports events across the globe are cancelled
Nurses are being recalled
Doctors are being recalled

The world is changing around us
What can we do
When we prayed, the fires subsided

Can all nations pray for mercy
Pray for forgiveness

We need to give 2 metres between humans
We need to not gather in small groups

This can go on for a very long period
What is happening to our world

Social Distancing

Composed at home on 20/03/20
Inspired to write about the social distancing

Race for Life #321

This used to be the famous slogan
Cancer Research
When we volunteered
We became familiar with the term
Race for life

Not thinking too deep about the meaning
There is nothing like it now as
Everyone is racing for life

The doctors are racing
The nurses are racing
Children are racing
Shopkeepers are racing to close their doors
Pubs are racing to close their doors

Everyone is in a race to save lives

Can we slow down and enjoy the moment
God has not given us a spirit of fear
We are anxious about what is happening around us
Can we all stop racing and see what happens

When we stop
God will start
Race for life

Composed at home on 23/03/20
Inspired to write about the race for life

Stay Safe #322 #Drivers #Riders

Drivers
Riders
Bikers

I was driving on the Bow Roundabout
I saw the red bus ahead of me
It had an interesting image of a rider
They looked out for the drivers
The drivers looked out for the riders

I thought that was very thoughtful
To have an advert like that

Reminding us to be there for each other
Reminding us to keep safe

As we drive on the roads
The Highway Code reminds us to do the same
The driving signs help us to drive safe on the roads
What have you done today to keep you safe
I have kept a good distance from the bus ahead of me

Drivers
Riders
Bikers

Composed at home on 28/03/20
Inspired to write about the bus

The Fireplace #323 #Warmth #Comfort

We went to the school event
It was in Orsett Hall
On our way out
Through the reception
The fireplace caught my attention

The detail on the mantle piece
The mirror above the fireplace
The fireplace

Made from marble stone
The fruits and the kings embedded in history

The bronze artefacts reminded me of the Chess game
The arch design of the fireplace was inviting me

The unlit log lying there, waiting to be lit; sooner or later
The queen's head on the corner of the mantle
The fireplace had so much beauty

You would want to lounge and relax on your sofa
Enjoy the warmth and comfort from the fire
Stay home stay safe
The fireplace

Composed at home on 31/03/20
Inspired to write about the fireplace

Big Thumbs Up Event #324

Essential key workers
The nurses and doctors
The support workers
Health care assistants

The bus drivers
The pharmacists
The shopkeepers

The employers decided to reward the employees
The Big Thumbs Up Event

The clapping across the nation
On a Thursday evening was fun
The employers ask us to log on at 11.00am on Yammer
To listen to our director

Buy pizza and cakes for all frontline workers
Post a photo of you with a thumbs up to say
Thank you for all you do for our residents

I thought that it was a nice gesture
From an employer towards their employees
The Big Thumbs Up Event

My staff enjoyed the event
Thank you

Composed at home on 04/04/20
Inspired to write about the event

Happy Easter #325

We spent the last two Easters in France
2018-2019
This year we are spending Easter in the UK

I do not have my Easter Eggs yet
My children look forward to Easter each year
Though they are adults now
They still look forward to their eggs
I normally get a few eggs for some family friends

I have taken Easter Eggs abroad before
I have given out eggs to the homeless
I have always enjoyed an Easter vacation

But this year is different
I look forward to the journey
On the train from Dover

I enjoy the four-hour drive from Calais
Our resort in Bailly-Romainvilliers

The walks on the grounds
Surrounded by nature
Peace and calm

The golf course
The local shops on the square
Carrefour

The local chocolate shop
The bakery on the square
The butchers in the corner

Our favourite restaurant
The ambiance and the locals
What is different this Easter for you

Happy Easter

Composed at home on 07/04/2020
Inspired to write about Easter egg

The Queen #326 #Message of Hope

At this time in Britain
The country was in lockdown for two weeks
Due to the COVID-19 pandemic
The country was in disarray

The country was more or less facing a challenging crisis
The Prime Minister of the UK was struck down by COVID-19
The Queen spoke to the nation
Over 24 million across the globe tuned in to see Her Majesty The
Queen
The Prime Minister has been in high spirits since leaving
Buckingham Palace

The Queen's speech was a message of hope to nations
It was unique and timely
We all needed to hear this from someone in her position
The message was reassuring

She thanked all the frontline workers
The doctors, the nurses, the carers
The bus drivers, the supermarkets
The cleaners, the chemist—amongst others

We will meet again
We will be together again
We will be with our friends again
We will be with our families again
A time will come when this will end

The Queen
A message of hope

Composed at home on 09/04/2020
Inspired to write about the Queen's message

Stop and Collect my Thoughts #327

It was Sabbath day
A Sabbath like none before
Before I would be abroad
Abroad in France—the last two years

A year ago I was different
Different to who I am today
Today I thought about a lot of things
Things that brought back memories

Memories of vacations in New York
New York I have enjoyed vacationing
Vacationing and sightseeing

Sightseeing took me to the memorial
Memorial of 9/11
9/11 was bad enough
Enough is enough

Enough of the dying populations
Populations decreasing by numbers
A high number of people dying
Dying from coronavirus
Virus known as COVID-19

COVID-19 led to prayers
Prayers for nations
Nations to heal themselves
They can heal from this epidemic
Epidemic of nations

Nations brought to a halt
Halt and a stop
Stop and collect my thoughts
Thoughts in disarray

Disarray can lead to prayers
Prayers for New York

Featured in Poetica 2 - Poetry Anthology 2020 January 2021
Composed in my room on 11/04/2020

The Map on the Cruise #328

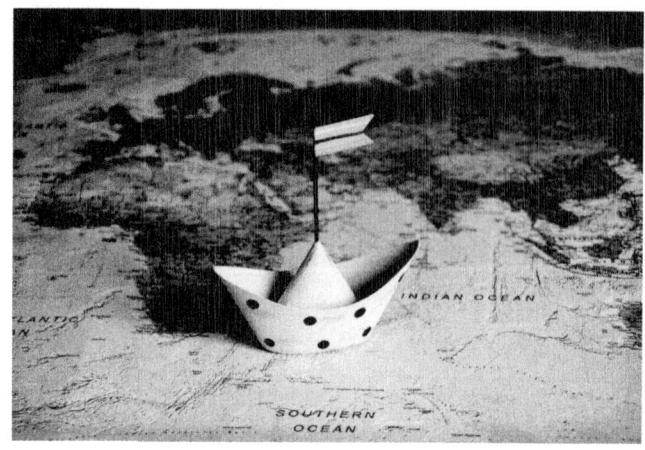

It was my hubby's 60th in May
We had planned to go on a Mediterranean cruise
We had made t-shirts for everyone

Friends and family were all booked up
From America, Nigeria and the UK
Until the coronavirus struck

We had bought gifts for everyone
Wine glasses for the men
Flasks and cereal bowls for the women

The coronavirus broke out so the cruise was postponed
The cruises spread the virus

The cruises became a place for the virus to spread
The cruises became a place no one wanted to be
The air in the cabins got recycled and no one wanted to go on a
cruise

I have enjoyed cruises with friends
This map was found on the Royal Caribbean

It caught my attention
With all the states in America
My favourite destination
My favourite vacation

I prayed for New York during the coronavirus crisis

The map on the cruise

Composed at home on 16/04/2020
Inspired to write about the map

One Man's Trash is Another Man's Treasure #329

'One man's meat is another man's poison'
'All that glitters is not gold'
'Make hay while the sun shines'
'Rome was not built in a day'
'When in Rome do as the Romans do'

These are all sayings I have grown up with
When you watch Treasure Hunt on TV
Some families dump things in the trash

A lady picks them up and makes something out of someone else's
trash

She gives the money to the families after she has made a profit
She gets someone to fix it and sells it online
It is interesting in life when you are passionate about something

It might not be someone's else 'cup of tea'
There goes the saying—'one man's trash is another man's treasure'
I am happy that I am making an impact with what I treasure

Tell me what you treasure in life

Inspired to write about the trash lorry
Composed at home on 17/04/2020

Lockdown Inspiration #330

I saw the plant daily on my table
It was from Mother's Day
Taking us into lockdown
Inspired me each time I looked at it
Working from home

Virtual daily meetings
Virtual interviewing
Writing my chapters
Writing my weekly prompts

That love of green
Made me realise there was more in life to live for
Despite all the deaths announced
I look at life before my eyes; the plant living in my living room

The ivy
The pink baby roses
The green plants
All bring a good vibe

Lockdown vibes
Lockdown inspiration
Spurs me to carry on
Life is for the living

Composed in my living room on 18/04/2020
Inspired to write about the plant

The Neighbour's Pet #331

I just arrived from work one day
As I came out of my car
I saw a furry cat in the neighbour's yard

They had a dog, I also know
She was cute
She had green eyes
She was black and grey
She stared at me with intensity

She did not blink
She kept her gaze
I was amazed at her bravery
She did not move and kept her pose

I decided to take a photo
I took out my phone
And yet she was there

So I composed this poem in the car
I took my shopping bags indoors
By the time I came back, she had gone
The neighbour's pet—I thought was cute

Composed at home on 22/04/20
Inspired to write about the neighbour's pet

Dogs Walking #332

It was our evening walk during lockdown
We saw the three dogs walking towards us
That brought some joy to my heart

I had a fear of dogs from a previous experience
However on this occasion my heart warmed towards the dogs

Most of my neighbours have dogs
Some have cats
I have always thought of having a pet some day
Perhaps when I am a lot older
You need the time and space to care for one

What's your favourite animal
Do you have a pet
What animal would you have as a pet

I have seen some strange creatures on television that serve as pets
We must maintain our pets—they provide good company
We must not neglect our animals or that will be seen as animal cruelty

Be kind to animals
Take them out on a walk
Like the dog walker just did !

Composed at home on 24/04/2020
Inspired to write about the dogs taking a walk

The Skip #333

We went on our morning walk
Social distancing and all
Crossing each time we saw a walker nearby
Jumping each time we saw the couple and their dog

The lady and her dog up the hill
I took a photo of her dog
The joggers, the couple
And one male jogger

As we walked past the Co-op
I saw the skip on the left in the courtyard
With the bath and all the clutter

The skip reminded me of a time that I was decorating
My two bathrooms early this year
My kitchen some years ago

We had to move the old to make room for the new
We had to rediscover our home again
As old things became new again
As we decluttered our home

A new season was upon us
As we replenished our home with new things
Old ways had passed

Declutter
Decorate
Discover
Replenish

The skip can take them all

Have you ever hired a skip?
What did you put in your skip?

Composed at home on 25/04/20
Inspired to write about the skip

House with Character #334 #Vibrance

We went on our usual walk
I saw the house on the left
I have walked this route for several months

I saw the sun on the brick wall
I saw the lamp shade above the number on the tiles
I saw the number on the white tiles
111
Reminds me of Spain as they love their tiles

The sun shape sends a positive message out to anyone
The house with character came to mind

The house had so much character
I thought to take a photo the first time

The next time I walked past
I thought I would write a poem about
The house with character
I wanted to know who lived in a house like this
Reminds me of the programme—The Keyhole

Who lives in a house like this
What peculiar things are in your home
What gives your house character
What could you not do without in your home

Composed at home on 28/04/2020:
Inspired to write about the house with character

103 Famous People #335

It was during lockdown
I went to post my parcels
Winners of book promotion

Kebab shop caught my attention
Saw the painting hanging
Very interesting images
Could not make sense of it

The shopkeeper did not speak much English
The colleague said it was the famous painting
My daughter googled it
103 famous people painted on the painting

Queen Elizabeth
Muhammad Ali
Michael Jordan
To mention a few

In the painting
My curiosity had paid off
I always ask questions
When I don't understand

Be curious and ask questions
You never know where it might lead you
On your journey

103 famous people

Inspired to write about the painting
Composed at home on 13/05/2020

Roses on the Brick Wall #336

On our evening walk
Same house on the right

Past Co-op on the right
Past the block of flats on the left
Past the junction on the right
Past the bins on the left

The brick wall reminds me of when you are moving so fast
And then you hit a brick wall
What do you do to go through the wall
What have you done to overcome writer's block

I don't force it
I let it flow when it wants to
It will come back to you
But if you hit a brick wall in life
It's different—you need to find a way around

The wall you cannot give up
The roses on the brick wall
In all its beauty

Remind me of growth
Despite the brick wall
We can all experience growth in our lives
We just need space to do just that

Growth
We all deserve it—growth

Inspired to write about the roses on the brick wall
Composed at home on 15/05/2020

Lockdown Celebrations #337

Celebration celebrations
Anniversary Anniversaries
Wedding Weddings
Matrimony Matrimonial

Twenty-eight years seemed like
Yesterday, Today
All those years gone
Twenty-five—I was then

Fifty-three she is now
Lockdown did not lock us down
Celebrations went ahead in lockdown

Birthday Birthdays
Cake cutting Cake slicing

Virtual celebrations
Guests online in lockdown
Lockdown could not get in the way
Two cakes on this match day

Sixty years has come by
Thirty-two when we got married
Makes him sixty today

Lockdown celebrations
Two weeks in lockdown
Two weeks on the struts
Lockdown celebrations
We mean to say

Composed at home on 18/05/2020
Inspired to write about the celebrations in lockdown

Bow Roundabout #338

Driving through daily
Lights stop daily
Traffic on A12 daily
Roundabouts daily
Bow Road daily

Bow to cars daily
Bow for drivers daily
Bow to Queen nicely
Bow tie event daily
Bow Roundabout

Means a lot lately
COVID-19 lately
Virus kills daily

5 minutes from work nicely
Reminds me to start work daily
Reminds me to strap up daily
Such a nice feeling daily

Bow Roundabout nicely
Bow Roundabout daily
Reminds me to be safe daily

Composed at work on 21/05/2020
Inspired to write daily

Lockdown Motivational Tips #339

Hand washing many times a day
2 metres social distancing apart
Self-isolate in your flats
Communal spaces closed off

Masking up in communal spaces
Full body suits if required
Goggles for water splashing
Shoe covers for feet protection
Aprons and gloves for personal care
Masks for medication administration

No contractors on site
Doctors and nurses wash your hands

Staff wash your hands
This has worked—there are no cases
In sight no cases on site

Masks in enclosed spaces
Drive and walk to work
Walk from home if you can
Don't use public transport

Drive to the sea front
Meet one family member 2 metres apart
Maintaining these steps
Will keep us in good health

Against COVID-19
Against coronavirus

These tips have helped everyone
Lockdown Motivational Tips

Composed at home on 22/05/2020
Inspired to write about the motivation tips

Haiku of Happiness #340

Joys and Hopes of the Seasons
Bring happiness to our hearts
Haiku of Happiness

Composed at home on 24/05/20
Inspired to write about Haiku

Haiku to the Black Man #341

Black cab and black man
Evening with calm and character
Prowess shone through man

Strength is his skill
Power, class and victory
Such a gentle kill

Social class a struggle
Perseverance and resilience
Yet he will survive and drive

Egoism and heroism
Martin Luther King, Obama
Nelson Mandela—a king

Women flock by
Yet he chooses his dream
And lives life as a dream

Energy defines him
Black man defines his path
As no one drives his fight

Black man inspiration
The lower of the life's class
Highest when he gets to class

Black Man Inspiration

Due to feature in Haiku Society Anthology 2021
Composed at home on 24/05/20
Inspired to write a Haiku for the black man

I Posted a Letter on our Walk #342

I saw a skip on our walk the other day
I saw a golf club in the skip—on Monday
I saw the lady walking the three dogs the night before—on Tuesday

We saw the ice cream van at the house at the junction on our walk—on Wednesday
We met the man with four cars on our walk on our anniversary—on Thursday
We met the woman by the letterbox on our walks—on Friday

We met the woman who walked her dog 🐕 the other day—on Saturday

We saw the four bags filled with books on our walk—on Sunday

We saw the house with the grey door ▤ on our walk—on your
birthday
We saw the house with white cars on our walk—on the evening of
the VE Day
We have seen so much happen on our evening walks

What's your favourite evening and why

Composed at home on 26/05/2020
Inspired to write about evening walks

Haiku for the NHS #343

Clapping Clapping
Doctors, nurses, cleaners
Care workers, porters

Holding Holding
Seventies oldies, indoors only
Underlying health only

Dying Dying
Grieving the loss, pick up the loss
Burying the dead

Heroes Sheroes
Saving lives on our doors
Treating lives on their oars

Shielding Shielding
Protecting their teams
Furloughing their streams

Working Working
Recalling the retired
Volunteering the retired

Testing Testing
Symptomatic, asymptomatic
Home test kits, drive through streets

Rainbows Rainbows
The rooftops on blue scrapers
Windows were lit up

Contact tracing
Symptoms tracking—Heroes and Sheroes
Wards are dwindling

Losses are lost
Lives are saved
Heroes and Sheroes

Composed at home on 28/05/20
Inspired to write for the NHS

Three Colts Lane #344

We sat We saw We conquered
All-inclusive picture

We care
We respect
We are inclusive

Are we
240 years ago
Three Colts Lane

I tread so many times

We care

Pub over 240 years

Land of cobbles

With underpasses

We respect

Such a timely poem

In our world today

We respect

1770

Local inn

Where a king was born

So much hate today

A son is lost on our streets

We care

A resident needs our care

Reception full of care

Seats in despair

We respect

We care

We are inclusive

We sat We saw We conquered

Composed at home in bed 30/05/20
Inspired to write about the picture Three Colts Lane

There is No Burden Too Heavy for Him #345

The man a dialogue for humanity
The man part of human race
The man the model of life

The man lay down his burden
At the feet of the Lord
Jesus carried the cross so that we may live

Life means nothing to anyone
The life that He lost to save humanity
Is taken on our streets to dehumanise

What a waste of life to humanity
Life's lost in broad daylight in humanity

Lay down the burdens at the foot of humanity
He can heal the human race from dehumanising acts of inequality

The violence on our streets cry out for humanity
What a shame for humanity

Looting criminalises all humanity
Peaceful protest is such a priority

Humanity can yell out in creativity
There is no burden too heavy for humanity

Created at home on 02/06/2020
Inspired to write about the burden of humanity

The Grey Door #346

What lies behind the grey door
This may sound cliche´
As grey is the new black
Fifty shades of grey

When things aren't clear
We say they are grey
It's always been the colour
With some drama

Grey is a favourite colour
It's cool and attracts
What lies behind the grey door
I guess we will never know

We have walked this path
So many times
The door is always shut
The house is empty
It's unfinished

The workmen reside there
The lights are always off
The skip on the driveway
The unfinished business

The grey door will be open
One day a family might move in
Then the grey becomes clear

There will be no more
What lies behind the closed door

Composed at home on 03/06/2020
Inspired to write about the grey door

The Three Headed Witch #347

The past behind
The present in her hand

Does she go or stay?
In the middle I will stay

The hat an icon of confusion I see

Inspired to write about the image
Composed on 17/10/2020

One More Journey #348

Is all George Floyd wanted
I can't breathe

One more Journey
He pleaded for mercy

One more Journey
Some cannot leave their homes
Shielding indoors
Closed malls
Closed restaurants

One more Journey
Beaches open
Parks are open
Essential travel only

One more Journey
Protesters on our streets

One more Journey
To drive change
To have an impact

One more Journey
I can't breathe
He begged but he was refused
Life

One more Journey
He wanted to breathe

One more Journey
Black lives matter

Composed at home in 07/06/2020
Inspired to write about one more Journey

The Bus Stop #349 #Arguments

The feeling of when you get on the bus and can't wait to get off
The feeling you get when the discussions become heated due to
COVID-19
The feeling you get when you feel your voice is not heard
The feeling you get when you have tried your best

It can happen to anyone and everyone—anywhere
The feeling you get when you feel you are being ignored
The feeling you get when there are tensions at work
The arguments during COVID-19 can be extensive

Sometimes you take a step back
Sometimes you don't get involved
Sometimes you may try and diffuse it

Arguments are not healthy
They can impact your health
Arguments should be avoided where possible
Try and sort things out before they lead to an argument

Have you been involved in an argument
Could that argument have been avoided

The bus stop ends the arguments as you get off and are no longer
involved

Composed at home
Inspired to write about the bus stop on 13/06/2020

Benefits of Working from Home #350

I have never known such a time when working from home became
a norm
I had known of flexible working arrangements
But this became mandatory
You had to work from home if you were an essential worker

It turns out that there was a pandemic
Before we realised we could all work from home
And achieve similar results

Reduction of congestion and traffic on our roads

Essential workers could travel into work sooner
And help the patients and lessen pressure on NHS
It would reduce the spread of the infection from transmitting

We could spend more time on Netflix
We could order more packages from Amazon
Parcels were being dropped off at two-metres distancing

We could be on our laptops and eat through the day
We missed our colleagues as we could only see them virtually
We missed catching up after work in bars
Or having lunch at the café
We missed popping into the shopping malls—window shopping

The benefits of working from home are great
As you spend more time on the sofa surfing on the web
You spend more time with family
Or you might actually become a teacher if you have young ones

You may end up with a baggage of depression
And sometimes it might mean not visiting anyone
If you breach the regulations you might end up being arrested

Would you still like to work from home
Are there benefits to working from home
Or are there hindrances to continue working from home

The choice is no longer yours
As you have been asked to work from home
The benefits of working from home is ludicrous

Composed at home on 14/06/2020
Inspired to write about the sign at the bus stop

The Apples 🍎 #351

You are the apple of my eye
You make me want to sigh
The beauty in your eyes
Can make me want to cry

The apple of my eye
Is the love in my life
Love is all you cry
28 years have been rewarding

The apple of my eye
Has been my man for sure
Granny Smiths are ripe
Cooking apples are tasty

The apple of my eye
Gala apples he likes
Braeburn apples I like
The apples of our lives

The apple of my eye
It's Father's Day—I like
I get to celebrate my life
With the apple of my eye

Happy Fathers Day to the apple of my eye

Featured in Stripes Magazine January 2021
Inspired to write about the apples
Composed on 19/06/2020 at home

The Sower #352

The green pears 🫗
In my local supermarket

The Parable of the Sower
You reap what you sow

We are all different
No two pears are the same
Some big, small, yellow, green

A growth journey
The seed is the gospel
The sower is the proclaimer

The first three soils
Represent rejection
The last acceptance

The more the seed
The less corruption
Alms, tithes, offering
And grace are ways of
Sowing as a Christian

The pears are a reminder
We can't give from an empty
Bucket, so we need to sow
And then we can reap
Good fruits

Featured in Stripes Magazine January 2021
Composed at home 🏠
Inspired to write about the pears on 21/06/2020

Sitting on the Fence #353

As I walk past each time
It reminds me of Marbella
The fences in the Guadamila Estates
I went in May last year

The image very vivid
The area is green and very affluent
Reminds me of Humpty Dumpty
Sitting on a wall
And the birds named Peter and Paul

Reminds me of me sitting on the fence sometimes
Can't make up my mind

Or at work sometimes can't make a decision
Of what to do and what not to do

Sometimes we have to make a leap of faith
What if you were on the fence and an animal was to attack
Would you carry on sitting or would you jump off the fence

That's what we have to do
We cannot carry on sitting on the fence
As we have to move for things to move

Sitting on the fence

Featured in the 2021 Annual Anthology June 2021
Composed in the bank in Stratford
Inspired to write about the fence on 22/06/2020

Alloy Wheel #354

Beautifies your rides
Uplifts your tides
Coasts along your drive
Makes you feel alive

Allows your drive
Fabricates the ride

Brings the world alive
Makes the circle thrive
Brings out the ride

The alloy wheel
Reminds me to strive

Reminds me to drive
Reminds me to fight

Inspired to write about the alloy wheel
On a drive
Composed at home on 23/06/2020

Welcome on Board #355

Welcome on board
As you board the cruise
The concierge welcomes you on board

As you embark on the ship 🛳 ♂
The staff welcome you aboard
When the pandemic struck
The passengers could not disembark

The coronavirus kept them on board
Until the pandemic was clear
The cruise could not embark

The passengers on Princess Diamond Cruises
Stayed on board for so long
Over 700 out of 3711 passengers were infected on board
14 people died as a result

Would you go on board a cruise
Will you be welcomed back on board soon

My husband's 60th cruise was cancelled
He had a virtual birthday on Zoom

Welcome on board

Composed in the car on my way from Coventry
Inspired to write about the sign on 25/06/2020

Epping Forest #356

As we drove towards Coventry
The green forest on both sides of the road
Visiting family from abroad
Not seen them a while due to lockdown

At the roundabout
There was a queue of traffic
So we turned left into the forest
We ended up at a beautiful location
Surrounded by green

Families having fun
Young people having picnics
Sitting on the grass in the sun

The pub on the hill was serving beer
Such a nice atmosphere
I felt like coming out to join the group
But we were on our way out

The roads were narrow
The beautiful forest known as Epping
Tucked away in the green
Epping Forest
Relaxing, calming and energising

Makes you unwind as you drive past
We found this by chance
It was tucked away in the woods
A must visit next time I am out and about

Inspired to write my first poem of the Poetry Marathon
June 27-28th (12 poems in 12 hours) every hour
Composed at home on 27/06/2020

The Pub on the Hill #357

Was at the roundabout I sighted this one
But the actual one was the one on the hill
The beauty of seeing a glass of
Had not been seen in lockdown

All pubs were shut
It was such an unusual sight
The ban has just been eased
I was surprised to see the

People had been locked up for 12 weeks
Need to let off steam
The football was on

In the gardens people were required to stay apart
But I did not see any of that

The psychologist says it's human behaviour
And we follow the crowds
But we could be breaching the rules

The Pub on the Hill

#PoetryHalfMarathon #12Poemsin12hours
#onepoemhour #upforthechallenge
Composed at home 10.19am 11 minutes on 27/06/2020
Inspired to write about the pubs opening in lockdown

Bournemouth #358

The beach 🏖 full to the brim
Umbrellas ⛱ full of colours
Summer is upon us
People want vacations

The outbreak of the virus is imminent
We need to keep 2 metres apart
Is this possible—at the beach it is unimaginable

We need to see the spikes in other countries
Where the lockdown has been eased off too quickly

What can we do to maintain our distance
What can we do to keep apart

Were humans designed to be apart
All we want to do is give each other a hug

Love is intimacy on the beach
Love is topless on the beach
Love is where people show off their bits
Love is life on the beach

Bournemouth

Composed at home on 27/06/20 as part of the Poetry Marathon
Inspired to write about the beach

Ricoh Roundabout #359

The Ricoh—we visited once before
The Coventry Rugby ground

The roundabout with a spiral
Always caught my attention
Each time I visited this little town

Friends have children in uni here
It's been an amazing journey up here
Been here on numerous visits
Sorting out differences

My experience in the church grounds
My first journey of poetry begun by visiting
This little town

There must be some attachment to Coventry
I have always thought
The memory of the Ricoh roundabout never fades

It reminds me of going up in space
In a spiral with no ending
Such a freedom of power, I thought

I think
I will remain in that space
The spiral roundabout

Composed at home 🏠 *on 27/06/2020*
Part of the Poetry Marathon. Inspired to write about the spiral roundabout

Church in the Burial Ground #360

I did a church challenge this year
Always had a fascination about churches
A seven-day motivation and gratitude challenge

Thought about making a video in the church grounds
Never thought it would happen
But then the opportunity arose

The church in the burial ground
Reminds me of life after death
We all have to depart one day

The grounds seemed peaceful
With all the deaths we had across the globe

Means death is imminent
We should prepare for it
One day it might strike unannounced

It's the memories people leave behind that
Keep us alive

I speak daily to my mum in my kitchen
I have her mug in there to remind me of her

What's your memory of death
Have you anyone who you miss dearly due to this

Unforgettable truth
Unfortunate truth
Unforgivable truth

We have to move on
Death occurs anytime

Composed at home on 27/06/2020
As part of the Poetry half-marathon
Inspired to write about the church in the burial ground

Positive Affirmations #361

Thought I had to surround myself with
Positive energy

Helps to keep me focused
Helps to remain open
Transparent

Attended the Authentic Women Webinar today
Reminds us to be courageous
To be self-aware
Own yourself
Be bold
Be courageous
Do not apologise for who you are

Be who God has called you to be
Use your authentic self to tell a story
Be a magnet
Be firm in your belief
Accept your identity
Walk in it

Go forth
And deliver the vision that God has for you

I am strong 💪

Composed at home on 27/06/2020
Inspired to write about the positive affirmation
Part of the Poetry half-marathon
Authentic women

New Ways of Shopping #362

New banking
New ways of posting
New ways in pharmacies
All these—I have experienced this week
In malls

Due to COVID-19
Everything seems to have changed in three months

Barriers to demarcate traffic
Signs everywhere as reminders
But are we complying
I would say not always

You are on your own
If you want to beat the virus
You have to adapt to the new ways

This is the new way of living
Due to coronavirus

The queues are off-putting
But this is the way forward
New ways; new lives

Composed in the car on 27/06/2020
Inspired to write about new ways of living
Poetry half-marathon

Solar Panel #363

Harold Wood roundabout
The swimming pool shut
The library shut

The graffiti on the library walls
The solar panels on the house
At the junction

We have looked into having solar panels
Our roof was not steep enough
Same with having a loft
Our roof was not steep enough

Reduction in energy bills
Converting sunlight into electricity
This can be used to power electrical loads

Have you solar panels at yours
Is it efficient
Is it cost effective
Has it made a difference

Composed in the car
Inspired to write about the solar panel

QE11 Bridge at Dartford Crossing #364

On our way to Canterbury
The bridge that connects Essex to Kent
The high bridge above River Thames

The same toll free gates some time ago
Now you pay Dartford Crossing toll online

The bridge is amazing—breathtaking views on both sides of the
bridge
The beauty of nature is apparent
The beauty of engineering is apparent

With all the bridge's misadventures
You sometimes worry
But this bridge takes us to Gatwick Airport
It takes us to Canterbury

On a journey of adventure
Just like any other bridge
Would take you on a journey
Of a lifetime

The QE11 Bridge at Dartford Crossing

Composed in the car on our way to Canterbury on 27/06/2019
Inspired to write about the bridge
Poetry half-marathon

Roadworks #365

Roadworks
What are your opinions about roadworks
They slow you down

If you breach the speed limit
You can be fined
And it can cost you points on your licence

Roadworks cause unnecessary traffic
Roadworks improve our roads
Maintenance costs can be expensive

Potholes can cause accidents
Roadworks are necessary to maintain our roads at all costs
Do you recall a time you've had roadworks

The noise pollution
It can be disturbing if you live in a quiet area
If they are working on the roads where you live

It can be noisy
In as much as roadworks are important to us
They can be inhibiting

Composed in the car on 27/06/2020
Inspired to write about roadworks on the way to Canterbury
As part of the poetry half-marathon

Train Tracks #366

The image of unending tracks
Has always been a delight
The tracks from Canterbury

Take you to Stratford Station
My son's uni for three years
We visited three accommodations

One on campus
Two off campus
We got to know the town inside out

What an amazing culture
The tracks seem unending
In both ways

Both directions
Looked like you had to keep moving
No matter the storm—keep going

The train station on the left
What amazing views have you come across on a train track
What's the furthest you have travelled on a train?

Composed in Canterbury as part of the poetry half-marathon on 27/06/2020
Inspired to write about train tracks

The Statue #367

The statue in Bristol
Was uprooted and dropped in the river
As it had a link to slave trade
Following George Floyd's death

The statues in London were boarded up
To protect them from damage and abuse
Some statues were removed to protect them
These are images we have been used to in our cities

Being molested by the protesters
Peaceful demonstrations
Negotiations that all lives matter

Statues or no statues
All lives matter
Our statues, our legacy, our communities

The statue in Canterbury

Composed in the car on 27/06/2020
Inspired to write about the statues
Poetry half-marathon

Fox Close 368

Walking on my journey
I saw Fox Close

I looked right
The road ends on a T-junction
About eight houses
In the close

Pondered on the word *fox*
Thought of foxes at night
On the drive

We live around the green
So foxes come out at night

Would be fun to have foxes in the close
Fox Close

What does this remind you of
I thought I would name it
Fox Close
T-junction

The road is closed to foxes now
What does this remind you of

Inspired to write about Fox Close
Composed at home on 30/06/2020

The Birthday Card #369

Have you known anyone who reached 100
The Queen of England will celebrate with you
And post you a congratulatory message and card

When it's your Diamond Wedding Anniversary—60th
Blue sapphire—65th and platinum—70th

My parents did not reach their 70's
A church member turned 100 during lockdown
We were all delighted and celebrated with him
We are thankful to know someone of that age

With complete faculty
Living a good life
Who can smile and have a chat with you
Would remember your name

Such a delight to have crossed paths with
A legend in my church community
I would love to be 100

We saw this card in Canterbury during our visit
We thought to buy it and celebrate with a friend
From our church community
The legend in our community

Do you know anyone who has turned 100
Did you celebrate with them

The Birthday Card

Inspired to write about the birthday card

Takeaways #370

More than enough food is produced globally
However, more than 820 million go hungry each year
This has declined gradually
but still world hunger is on the increase
and affects 11% of people globally

When you see a sign like this in Canterbury
What comes to your mind
An image of a malnourished child on our screens
Reminding us to donate and support a charity like UNICEF

But this was a sign inviting us to buy takeaway?
Why is that—you wonder
Because of the pandemic, we can only have takeaways

But this will not be changing too soon
Takeaways seem to be increasing
With Uber drivers and Uber eats
Flooding our streets

Would you go without food to see what it feels like
Or would you rather pop in for a takeaway
Have you fasted before as part of your religion
Would you be inviting anyone hungry
For some food on our streets

Takeaways are here to stay
Come in if you are hungry

Composed at home on 03/07/2020
Inspired to write about the takeaway sign

Launch to the World #371

Rebirth is all we want
At Barking Creek

The clouds launch the blue skies
Above Valence House—the museum

The renewal of the Spotty Dog Pub at the corner
Strengthens our bond as a group in our communities

We continue to affirm one another
As we Rebirth to the Universe

Composed at the Barking Foxes Poetry Group
Inspired to write about new words

The Nude Couple #372

This challenged my view of my body
This gave me confidence in a human form
We are who we are
We owe it to ourselves to be who we are

We are created in God's own image
We are meant to be proud of who God made us to be

This couple in their nudity reminded me of who I am
When I was born I came into the world with nothing
We acquire layers that have been put on us by others

We have to be who we are
Who God designed us to be

Be proud of our bodies
Be proud of who we have become
Be proud to say no to any layers
Be proud to be on a nude beach 🏞 one day

The nude couple reminded me of who I was
Created in God's own image
Our bodies are the Temple of God
We must treat them as that

The Nude Couple

Composed at home on 11/07/2020
Inspired to write about the nude couple

Myself in a Beautiful Poem #373

Once broken
But now gifted
She uses her words as an
Arrow

Imagination is indescribable
Loves her energy
She is driven
Charismatic
Adorable

Jealousy her greatest enemy
Strength her greatest asset

Faith—her weapon

Inspired to write about myself
Composed at home on 12/07/2020

Thrilling #374

Towering higher
Intertwining to the sky
The higher thriller

Inspired to write a Haiku about The Tower
Composed at home 🏠 on 12/07/2020

Broadway #375

Walking down the high road
The brightness of the colours
The beauty of art on our streets

The pinks, blues and greens
Shocked to my eyes
Unknown to me as I always walk by

The moment of truth in my eyes
In our communities reminds me of Camden
Inviting you for a drink

The hustle of our high street
The communities back to life
The pandemic on our streets

The life in our midst
Is beautiful to see once again
Broadway is beaming with life once again

Broadway

Inspired to write about the bright colours on our streets
Composed at home on 14/07/2020

Tree of Life #376

Tree of life
Is a symbol of personal growth
Personal development
Our uniqueness
Individual beauty

As branches grow upwards to the sky
We grow stronger searching for greater knowledge
Wisdom and experiences as we move through life

The sign represents different things to different cultures and
religion
It is a sacred symbol
Carries different meaning in
Spiritual and religious philosophies

Represents immortality and eternity
Knowledge
Strength
Wisdom
Protection

So much meaning entangled in one symbol
What does the symbol mean to you
For me—personal growth

Inspired to write about the tree of life
Composed at home on 15/07/2020

Road Trip #377

Road trip to Calais
On our way—me, my hubby
Daughter and son

Off on holiday
Down to the green scenery
From Dover always

On the train we go
Or on the boat we sail through
Or we drive away

The tall wind vanes move
The sunflowers I have seen
Lovely cottage views

Arrive in Paris
Bailly-Romainvilliers
10 minutes away
Disneyland Paris

Carrefour—our store
At the town centre
Our road trip was fun

Your road trip could be fun too
Trip of a lifetime

Road trip

Composed at home on 16/07/2020
Inspired to write about the road trip

Las Vegas #378

Services open
The M1 to Northampton
Las Vegas—hurray

The vending machines
The turntable for money
Punters in hiding

MGM effect
Treasure Island—pirates show
The Palladium

Reminders of me
Vegas the strip with value
Money all around

You have to play to
Win or lose your willpower
The brave will survive

Been to Las Vegas
What's your favourite memory
Mine is the vending

The atmosphere
Vibrant with lights and colours
Vegas for anyone

Composed at home on 18/07/2020
Inspired to write about the vending machines Las Vegas

Twin Mushroom #379

The omelette with eggs
Mushrooms peppers and spices
Mix well and stir up

The mushroom sliced
The heads cut up and chopped fine
The fryer sizzling

Twin mushroom I see
Never seen twin mushrooms before
Into the fryer

Siamese twins
Joined at the top but
Abundance I feel

Sounds strange I believe
How on earth did it happen
Twin mushrooms on earth

When next you fry
Think of the twin mushroom before you try
We need to know why

Twin mushroom

Composed at home on 21/07/2020
Inspired to write about the twin mushroom

Hanukkah #380

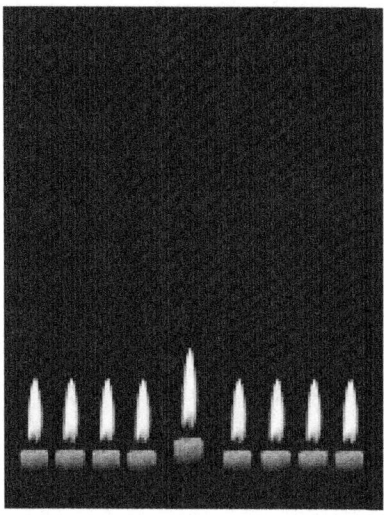

Hannukah—an eight day Jewish festival
From 25th December—Kislev
Celebrates rededication of the temple
In 165BC by the Maccabees
After its desecration by the Syrians

It is marked by the successive kindling of eight lights
It is also referred to as Feast of Dedication
Festival of Lights
Feast of the Maccabees

The Jewish Festival that begins on the 25th
This is according to the Gregorian calendar

My first contact with Hanukkah was my visit to Israel
I bought it from the church of God from a child
Who took a picture with me
I understand it was significant for children
To sell goods during pilgrimages to Israel

I am delighted with my Hanukkah purchase
What is your memory of a Hanukkah today?

Composed at work on 22/07/2020
Inspired to write about the Hanukkah

Dominoes Floating #381

Have you ever played Dominoes
What do you understand about the game
Tiles with black dots looking like a dice

The object of keeping them upright
You hate to drop them on their sides

I can't really recall how to play Dominoes
I learnt how to play this game a while ago
Yet when I stumbled upon it
It came flooding back like a drill in your head

I thought to write a poem, as the Dominoes
Were not just floating in water
They were up against a skyscraper

A hand grabbing to pick them up
Before they drop too deep into the sea
A hand holding on despite the pebbles in the sea

It's like when you drop a precious ring
And you have to find it

What does your memory of the game Dominoes mean to you
Mine means a lot to me as it brings back a memory
I would never want to fade away

But the memory of the game Dominoes
Brought this back to my mind
The Floating Dominoes on the skyscraper
An excellent image for anyone

Composed at home on 26/07/2020
Inspired to write about the floating Dominoes

I Remember #382

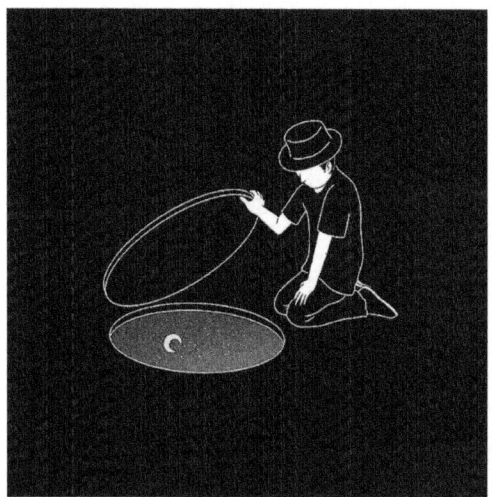

I
I remember
I remember a
I remember a time
I remember a time when
I remember a time when I
I remember a time when I celebrated
I remember a time when I celebrated my
I remember a time when I celebrated my birthday

I
I went
I went on

I went on a

I went on a cruise 🚢

We

We flew

We flew to

We flew to Abu Dhabi

We

We sailed

We sailed to

We sailed to Oman

I

I went

I went to

I went to the

I went to the mosque 🕌

I

I met

I met a

I met a Chinese

I met a Chinese boy 👦

I met a Chinese boy and

I met a Chinese boy and took a

I met a Chinese boy and took a photo

We
We stopped
We stopped at
We stopped at Falmouth
We stopped at Falmouth and
We stopped at Falmouth and went
We stopped at Falmouth and went to
We stopped at Falmouth and went to the
We stopped at Falmouth and went to the market

We
We visited
We visited the
We visited the first
We visited the first church
We visited the first church 🏠 in
We visited the first church in Jamaica

I remember a time when I celebrated my birthday
I went on a cruise
We flew to Abu Dhabi
We sailed to Oman
I went to the mosque
I met a Chinese boy and took a photo
We stopped at Falmouth and went to the market
We visited the first church in Jamaica
I remember

Composed at home on 31/07/2020
Inspired to write, using 'I remember' and 'Birthdays' as a theme
for the Barking Foxes Group

Freelancer #383

Was searching for an illustrator
For my new poetry book
I went onto the writers group
Was advised to try Fiverr
Had a terrible experience

Someone in the group suggested Freelancer.com
What a beautiful experience compared to Fiverr
Put my cover request into a contest for six days
All the freelancers were submitting
Their designs for my cover

I was awarding them stars based on my interest
I felt sorry when I rated some twos

I did not give up
There were about 53 entries
At the last minute I was caught between two entries

Suddenly this entry came up at the last minute
That was my entry
An illustration of all the different hobbies in my book
I was mesmerised, delighted—loved it
I accepted the entry

We had to work on perfecting
The entry to my required standard
The freelancer was excellent
I would recommend
Freelancer

Would you use them for your book cover?
What has your experience been?

Composed in the car on 09/08/2020
Inspired to write about freelancer experience

First Day Back #384

It was the first day back
We had been indoors for months
April, May, June and July

It all seemed strange to go back out there
Not confined in a car
It felt surreal and I missed the outdoors

The commute to work
Mixing with other passengers on the train
On the bus and walking in the malls

First day back
We sat two metres apart
We stood two metres apart on the platform
We wore our masks on the train

The car park had changed at the station
The parking bays were now marked
Everything seemed surreal

First day back
The car space had new wooden frames
The road had been tarred
The road had been marked

Everything seemed different
The first time on the bus in four months
I drove to work since the pandemic
The first time on the bus

The oyster spot was sealed
The driver's compartment was sealed
The seats were sealed

I sat on my own
The space next to me empty
No one sat next to me
The journey seemed weird
But I was glad to be there

My first takeaway in ages
My favourite kebab joints
I could not resist it
The queues were familiar
Yet we stood two metres apart

First day back
I was back—I was happy to be back
I stood in the shade under the tree
I felt alive again
I could give more
I could receive more

First day back
On the train
On the bus
In the kebab shop
The first day back
Would I change it for another?

Composed at home on 06/08/2020
Inspired to write about the first day back

Appetite for Life #385

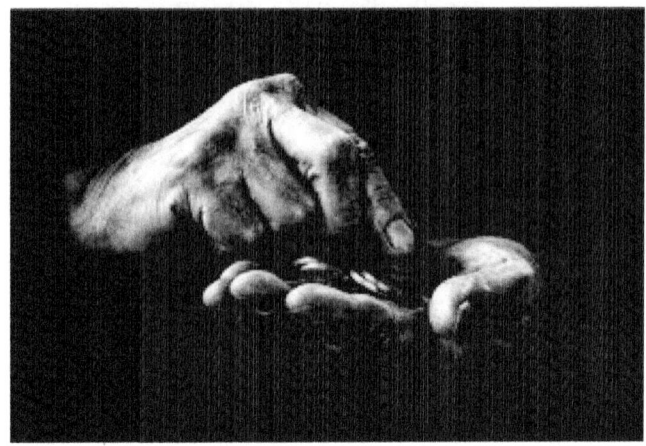

Happened on the way to Coventry
At the services
We stopped for KFC

Then I saw the writing on the wall
It inspired me to write about life
The survivors

The deaths in millions
The zeal to want to survive
The zest to want to excel

In view of all that is happening around you
The tenacity to want to do well
The appetite of life

Reminded me that we are here to achieve
We are here not to exist
But to have dominion

God has given us all we need
God will see you through
The Journey of Life

The Appetite for Life
What does this remind you of
What does this remind you to do

Composed at home on 13/08/2020
Inspired to write about appetite for life

Red Poppies #386

One evening on our walk
Facing writings talk
Been on this route

Saw the yellow poppies
Then the red poppies
These were not usual poppies

They looked like balls
They seemed beautiful

These red poppies
Reminded me of other red poppies

They are beautified in our street
They inspired our walk

It was the walk of kindness
The red poppies became a part of that
I had not seen a plant like this before

Red poppies
What does this remind you of
Does it bring back memories

Red poppies

Inspired to write about the red poppy plant
Composed at home on 14/08/2020

Sunset on the Beach #387

Sunset on the beach
Sunshades ditched on the beachfront
Gazing at the sun

Lovers stand still
Sunset stands still
Sunset beach stands still

Sands—fun and fine
Sand and shells on the seashore
Sandy and sunny

Lovers catch a glimpse

Lovers having fun in the moment
Lovers stand in awe

Inspired to write at home about the sunset
Composed at home on 16/08/2020

Four Shades of Seven #388

We had not seen each other in months
We met up in the mall
It was a sunny afternoon

There was hustle and bustle
The kids were on break
The weather was nice

We had time to chat
We spoke about so much
Within the hour

We touched on our children

The present; the future
The pandemic effect on us

The need to be there to support each other
One of us had lost their dad
The need to support her

I saw a foster carer I knew
With her teenage daughter
It was wonderful

It filled me with so much joy
I shared my joy outwardly
As I walked

I saw the number seven
In the window display in four different views
I thought I could write about the number

Seven has been a different number
My birthday has a seven
I had a terrific seven years

I understand the number seven is significant
Four shades of seven
What does seven signify for you?

Does it bring back good memories?

Mine is mixed feelings
The four shades of seven

Inspired to write about seven
Composed at home on 20/08/2020

Cloud Drops #389

The clouds in the sky
The views from the window
The views on the rooftop

The sky looked amazing
The sun was setting
The light caught my attention
It was divine to watch the views

The moment when you imagine
The clouds in pockets
Seemed they were dropping from the sky
Onto the rooftops

I took a photo with my daughter
And called it
The cloud drops on the rooftop

What has inspired you to write
Have you written about a cloud ☁

Inspired to write about the clouds
Composed at home on 20/08/2020

Tower of Tops #390

The cylinder of power
The Tower full of colour
The tops full of variety

The image with a difference
The decor that appeals

The tops on the bottle tops
The metal steel of colour
Manufactured for bottles
Fanta, Coca-Cola, Sprite
My favourites

The Tower has so many
The colours were prestigious

The colours vibrant
The colours of creativity

How many tops stood so strong
The beauty of an artist
Sitting or standing strong
As a Tower

Tower of Tops

Inspired to write about the tops
Composed at home on 21/08/2020

The Golden Triangles #391

The shoppers step off
The escalator at the end
The two floors packed
Children out and about

The triangles dotted in gold
Hanging from the ceiling
New on the horizon
Not been here in eight months
First time this year

It was a new decor
That hit you right in the eye
The golden triangles

Brought glamour
Brought beauty
To the mall
For the shoppers to enjoy a day out

The golden triangles made my day
What were your highlights of your day?
Were they plated in gold?

Composed at home on 21/08/2020
Inspired to write about the golden triangles

Spiral World #392

I went to Lakeside on a day out
It was a nice day out with my daughter
I like arts and artefacts
I saw the works on display

The bowls and dishes
I took a photo of the dish
It was circular in shape
It was designed in spheres
It had a shape at the centre

It reminded me that we are all stars
At the centre of the world
We are all connected with countries
We are all connected with languages

We can unite as a star
Shining bright at the centre of the world
The star can do amazing things
It shines bright at night in a dark sky

You can be the star in a spiral world
Shine your light in a spiral world
Wherever you are

Inspired to write about the dish
Composed at home on 25/08/2020

Food Pod #393

I hadn't been to Lakeside this year
It was August 2020
A place I visited every month
My children knew this when growing up

I always loved Lakeside
The shops, the people
The buzz in the environment

We visited the food court
Normally packed with diners
The seats were sealed off
I sat on the high seats
My daughter went to get the meals

As I sat, I saw the red pod in the distance
The pod reminded me of when I was at
Work in my head office
They had pods

But this was a food pod
For diners to eat
In their privacy

It was exclusive because
It was in a food court
Not in a restaurant

I am used to seeing this in TGIF
Or Pizza Hut
Is this the new way of
Dining in a pod in the outdoors

Food Pod

Has this amazed you
What's your good journey been like
What has made your day or intrigued you

Inspired to write about the Food Pod in the food court
Composed at home on 26/08/2020

Tortillas #394 #Nachos

I have always liked nachos
I also love tortilla crisps
I was enjoying a day with my daughter

We came across the tortilla shop
We ordered some tortilla
With Guacamole sauce
Cheese and jalapeño

I have had some tortilla in Las Vegas
Fremont Street

I have had different nachos in
Giraffe's Restaurant
I have had a nice tortilla in
Harvester Restaurant
Nachos in Nando's is alright

But I love my tortilla even in the cinema
I have had some nachos with the red sauce
And onions

Where have you had your best tortilla
What made it special for you
I will always love tortilla nachos
They make my day any day

Inspired to write about tortilla
Composed at home on 27/08/2020

Pretzels #395

What's your favourite pretzel
My first knowledge of pretzels
Was when George Bush
Had a pretzel in his throat
I have since loved pretzels
When I am vacationing I have cinnamon flavoured

Pretzels
They come in different flavours
I was in Westfield the other day
I had a pretzel with cinnamon
I was in Lakeside
I had a pretzel with my daughter
What's your favourite pretzel?

Vanilla flavour
Sesame seeds flavour
Parmesan cheese
Chocolate flavour
Nutella hazelnut
Classic salted
Toffee sauce
Pretzel pizza
Pretzel bites
Pretzel sticks

It's amazing what you can do with a pretzel
What's your favourite pretzel?

Composed at home on 31/08/2020
Inspired to write about pretzels

New Beginnings #396

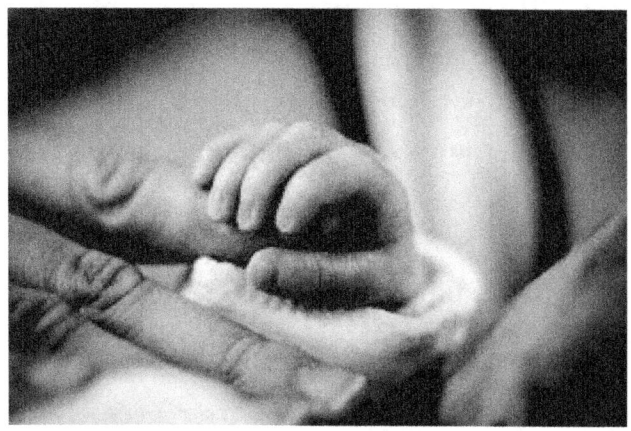

And the ease-down began
Shops opened
Restaurants with takeaways
Hairdressers
Nail parlours with shields
Dentists had new measures

GPs worked with PPE
Restaurants had 50% off
Gyms had new procedures
Trains were modernised
Platforms changed

This was a new beginning
Children went back to school

Churches reopened
Buses had new laws

Everything seemed new
It was the beginning of a new era
Vacations were different
Flying with masks
Quarantine for 14 days on arrival

This was a new beginning
That would take a while to get used to
A new beginning for our future

A new way of living
A new beginning that has changed the world we live in
We were not prepared for this change to our lives

But now we can move forward
And make a start
Take a step, a new beginning

A new direction for you and me and everyone
A new beginning to our world of living
A new beginning

*Composed at home on 02/09/2020 for Patsy Middleton's poetry
showcase
Inspired to write about new beginnings*

The Cafe #397

It was on my day off
My daughter asked me to the shops
She wanted to spend time with me

We went to the car wash
We stopped at the bank
She bumped into her mate

She asked if we could pop into the cafe
I hadn't been in one for a while
I have always liked cafes

The one in Romford, Barking, Chadwell Heath

They served all-day breakfast in all
My favourite is a mushroom and cheese omelette
With salad and fries

My daughter had a full English Breakfast
With tomatoes, onion rings,
Baked beans, mushroom, sausage, egg and toast

We bonded over brunch
It was nice to spend some time in the cafe
With my daughter

What's your cafe experience been like?
Where is your favourite cafe?

Composed at home on 07/09/2020
Inspired to write about the cafe experience

Feather #398

As smooth as silk
As soft as a pillow
As special for an occasion
As pretty as a peacock
As spikey as a hedgehog
As spooky for the dead

A sign of a loved one close by
Seen in special places
Worn on special occasions
Part of a living being
Sign of a deceased person
Made into fabrics and designs

A feather is such a pleasurable delight
To decorate hats

Composed at the Barking Foxes group
Inspired to write about the feather on 04/09/2020

Pirate Show #399

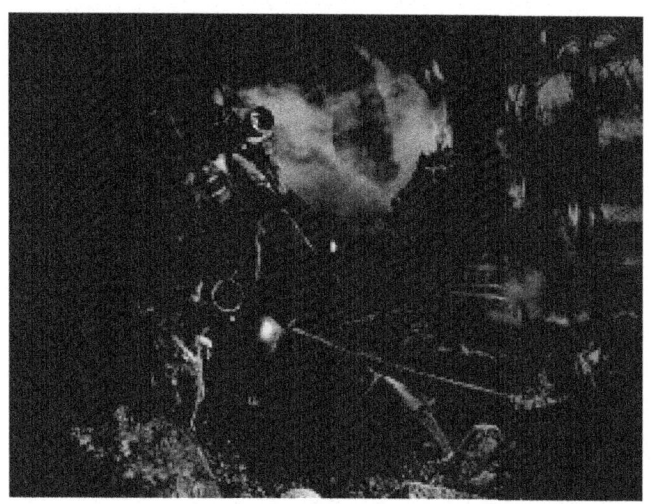

It was on a day out with my daughter
At the local cafe in Romford
They had a sign with a pirate 🏴☠️ evening
In the month of September
This happened to be the birthday month
For my daughter

It reminded me of the pirate show in
Las Vegas
Where we stopped and watched on the foot bridge
Treasure island
It was called
Such an amazing show
A must see for anyone visiting Las Vegas

Have you seen a pirate show before
Have you dressed up as a pirate as a child
What memories of a pirate does this poem bring up for you
Pirate Show

Composed at home on 08/09/2020
Inspired to write about the pirate show

Time #400

Time waits for no one
God is the master planner
He has a plan for each and every person

Have you heard of a time
When someone said for God to freeze time
Chadwick Boseman said that
We have limited time
We have to factor things in life
We can achieve as much success
But we cannot stop the days
The weeks, the months, the years
Have gone by

I was 23—forty years ago
It seems like yesterday
I graduated in 1988
I got married 28 years ago
Everything seems so close yet so far
My children are all adults

I have got to live and let live
I have got to leave my mark here on earth
I have got to leave a living legacy here
I have got to know deep in my heart
I did my best

Time waits for no one
Can we pull back wasted years
Can we rewind the clock ⏰
What is your understanding of time?

Inspired to write about time
Composed at home on 10/09/2020

About the Author

Sabinah Adewole is a member of the Barking Foxes poetry group, the National Poetic library UK, a member of the Society of Authors UK ,the Haiku Society of America and the Christian independent Publishing Agency -CIPA. Some of her poems appear in Stripes magazine in 2021. she won the International Poetry contest in 2020. She featured in the Havering daily mail and in Write on magazine in 2020. She started to write from a park bench in May 2018.

She has Eight published books,five best sellers and four self published. Some of her work can be found on Vocal Media and The Talent Bank. She has won several Poetry awards globally and she is well acknowledged on the Poetry circuit. She also teaches Poetry for beginners on her Sabìnah Poetry Online Classes.

This is her first series in this edition of -Sabìnah's Poetry - Her Travels (Travel Poetry)

Written during the Pandemic February 2020 - September 2020.

Her Writing

She has been greatly inspired by the gift of poetry and writing. She was gifted the gift of poetry while sitting on a park bench in Gidea park in May 2018. I have continued to write daily and have created over 700 poems some Children books, Faith book and Adults inspiration and Transformation poetry. She has co authored in four Anthologies and three Poetry Anthology this brought her into contact with coaches, publishers and a host of authors. She has Eight published books, five best sellers and six self published. Sabìnah completed her first Half Poetry Marathon in June 2021. She would like to share her Poetry with the world.

Published books

Journeys of Life Inspiration and Transformation Poetry Vol 1

Journeys of life Inspiration and Transformation Poetry Vol 2

Journeys of Life Inspiration and Transformation Poetry Vol 3

A Childs Journey Through Poetry - Fun, Inspiration and Adventure- Vol 1

A Childs Journey Through Poetry -Hobbies, Skills and Talents -Vol 2

Journey of a Childs faith based on Bible Stories - Vol 1

A Day on a journey to Lakeside Shopping Mall - Parenting and Families

My Memoirs -Empowerment Defiance

Printed in Great Britain
by Amazon

49094807R00119